# Time Jumpers

# FAST-FORWARD TO THE FUTURE

by
**WENDY MASS**

illustrated by
**ORIOL VIDAL**

SCHOLASTIC INC.

# Read all the

# Time Jumpers

## adventures!

scholastic.com/timejumpers

# Table of Contents

*For Dad, who finally let me show him how this thing called "The Internet" works! —WM*

*To my daughter, who likes sci-fi stories —OV*

Text copyright © 2019 by Wendy Mass
Illustrations by Oriol Vidal copyright © 2019 by Scholastic Inc.

Library of Congress Cataloging-in-Publication Data

Names: Mass, Wendy, 1967- author. | Vidal, Oriol, 1977- illustrator.
Title: Fast-forward to the future / by Wendy Mass ; illustrated by Oriol Vidal.
Description: First edition. | New York, NY : Branches/Scholastic Inc., 2019.
Series: Time jumpers ; 3 | Summary: This time a strange flashing cube from the magic suitcase sends them to a nearby city, Hadenstown, in the future, and they find themselves surrounded by flying cars, tall glass buildings, and robots; but Randall is also there, and the two children must scramble to figure out just what the mysterious cube is and get it back where it belongs—and their quest brings Chase face-to-face with his future self, Professor Teslar.
Identifiers: LCCN 2018035369| ISBN 9781338217421 (pbk) | ISBN 9781338217438 (hardcover)
Subjects: LCSH: Time travel—Juvenile fiction. | Robots—Juvenile fiction. | Magic—Juvenile fiction. | Adventure stories. | CYAC: Time travel—Fiction. | Robots—Fiction. | Magic—Fiction. | Adventure and adventurers—Fiction. | LCGFT: Action and adventure fiction.
Classification: LCC PZ7.M42355 Fas 2019 | DDC 813.54 [Fic]
—dc23 LC record available at https://lccn.loc.gov/2018035369

10 9 8 7 6 5 4 3 2 1                    19 20 21 22 23

Printed in China   62
First edition, March 2019
Illustrated by Oriol Vidal
Edited by Katie Carella
Book design by Sunny Lee

# The Noisy Night

**Chase** bolts upright in bed. What is making so much noise? Why are his bedroom lights flashing in the middle of the night?

He'd been dreaming about the suitcase. Right now, it was buried under a pile of stuffed animals in his sister's closet. But in his dream, all the weird objects inside it had come to life and flown around his room!

It has only
been a few days
since Chase and
his sister, Ava, got
the strange suitcase
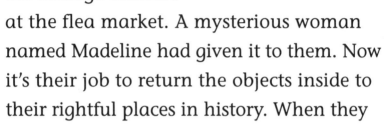
at the flea market. A mysterious woman
named Madeline had given it to them. Now
it's their job to return the objects inside to
their rightful places in history. When they
touch any of the stolen
objects, they travel
through time! They've
already visited 1920s
Egypt and medieval
England and helped
save history *twice*.

*Hiss! Shkree! La la la!*

Chase's clock radio starts blasting out a combination of music and static. He grabs for the knob, but it won't turn off!

Ava appears in the doorway, clutching the suitcase. She shouts, "What's going on?"

Chase joins her in the hallway. Lights blink on and off as they dash downstairs. The television keeps switching between channels, and the printer is spitting blank pages across the room.

"Don't worry, kids," their mom says as she rushes past them. "Dad is calling the electric company!" She disappears into the kitchen.

Ava suddenly gasps. "Chase! Look!" She holds out the suitcase. Golden light is pouring out from all sides! It definitely hasn't done *that* before!

They kneel behind the couch.

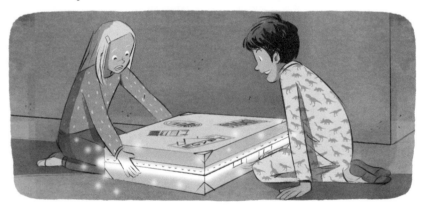

Chase flips open the lid. The small gold cube in the first row pops out of its slot and lands in the middle of the living room! It had been a dull golden color before, but now it's too bright to look at!

"What's *this*?" their mom asks, stepping into the living room. She reaches down for the cube.

Chase and Ava scramble out from behind the couch. "Stop, don't touch it!"

But it's too late.

Chase knows any second now his mom will travel back in time, to wherever the cube needs to go. She can't go alone! He and Ava lunge for Mom's legs and hold on tight.

## chapter 2

# Backward and Forward

**"Um,** what are you two doing?" their mom asks with a puzzled expression. Chase and Ava slowly open their eyes.

"Huh?" Ava says, looking around the living room. "We're still here?"

"Where else would you be?" their mom asks.

Chase swallows hard as he stands up. How can he tell her they'd expected to be sent back in time? She must not be a Time Jumper like them!

Mom shakes her head. "I'm too tired to figure you guys out right now." She looks down at the glowing cube in her hand. "Is this a new toy of yours?"

"Sort of?" Chase says. He feels bad not telling her the truth, but he and Ava agreed to keep their time travel a secret.

Mom tries to hand the cube to Ava, but Ava backs away. Chase does the same. They can't touch it and risk disappearing right in front of their mom! Plus, they want to be prepared for their trip this time. They don't want to time travel without their supplies.

Mom shrugs and places the gold cube on the couch. "I'm going to see if Dad reached the electric company. Go back to sleep."

Who could sleep with the house going crazy? Plus, they have a cube to send back in time.

After their mom leaves the room, Chase scoops up the cube with the bottom of his pajama top, careful not to touch it. Ava grabs the suitcase and follows him up to his room. The ceiling light is still flickering.

Chase grabs his hat and his bag where they'd stuffed snacks, water, money, and a small first aid kit. He plucks the remote control from the suitcase and sticks it into his bag. They'll need that to return to their own time. Then he pushes the suitcase under his bed.

"Ready?" he asks.

"One second," Ava says. She dashes out of the room. When she returns, she has her camera hanging around her neck. "Now I'm ready."

They grab hands. The i̶̶ ̶̶ ̶̶ Chase picks up the cube, all the electrical things that had been flashing and beeping suddenly stop!

"Whoa! Do you think this *cube* made everything go crazy?" Ava asks.

Chase tries to nod, but the spinning has started. There's something different about it this time. The images swirling around them are of strange places and objects. Are they spinning in a *different direction*?

# Welcome to the Future

## chapter 3

**When** the spinning stops, Chase and Ava find themselves lying on the ground, staring up at a tall bronze statue.

"Hadenstown? We've been to Hadenstown before!" Chase exclaims as he shoves the no-longer-glowing cube into his pocket. "We're not too far from home."

Ava jumps to her feet. "It sure didn't look like *this* last time!"

RICHARD HADEN
FOUNDER
OF
HADENSTOWN

Chase gets up and looks around. A sleek silver train whizzes overhead, winding its way between tall glass buildings. People wearing colorful jumpsuits walk on moving sidewalks.

And there are flying cars! Well, more like *gliding* cars, because they're only a few feet off the ground, but still! Nearly every person has a *robot* with them! One short, round robot just pulled an ice-cream cone out of its belly!

Now Chase understands why the spinning felt different — they weren't going *back* in time, they were going FORWARD.

They're in the future!

"I need to sit down," he says. Instantly, a chair springs up from the ground and scoops a surprised Chase onto it!

Ava laughs. "I wonder if that works for everything in the future." She takes a breath and shouts, "I need some cotton candy!"

But no cotton candy pops up from the ground.

"At least we know what year we're in." Chase points to a billboard.

GREETINGS, BOB!

Hadenstown thanks you for picking up after your neighbor's dog. That's three good deed points! Your total for the year 2121 is now eighty points!

The image changes as each new person walks past. The next person — a teenage girl — gets two points for being early to school.

"People must get points for doing good deeds," Ava says.

"I could watch that sign all day," Chase says. "But we have to find out why the cube brought us into the future."

A boy glides by on flying roller skates. He looks Chase and Ava up and down before skating away.

"We need to change out of our pajamas," Ava whispers.

"Yes, we need to blend in before Randall shows up," Chase adds. "And he *always* shows up!"

Randall — the angry man with different-colored eyes — has repeatedly tried to stop them from returning the objects from the suitcase to where they belong. Chances are, Randall's not far behind now.

"I don't think we can just borrow clothes like we did when we traveled to the past," Chase says. "What if people have security cameras inside their eyes? They could be recording our every move and arrest us for stealing."

"We'll have to find a clothing store," Ava says. "Good thing we brought money with us."

They start walking, but they don't get far before the boy on the flying skates doubles back toward them. He's waving his arms and shouting. "Look out! Move!"

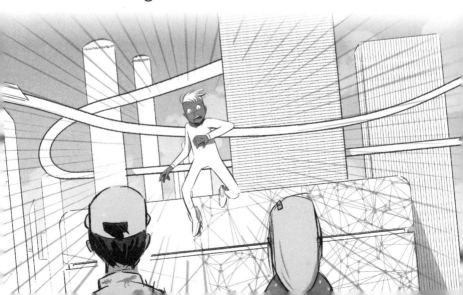

# Look Out!

## chapter 4

**Chase** and Ava barely have time to leap to the side before a flying car lurches to a stop inches away from them. The back door opens and out hops Randall!

"Give me the cube," Randall demands, thrusting out his hand.

"Your car almost hit us!" Ava shouts back.

He glances at the car. "Yeah, guess these flying cars aren't totally perfected yet," he says, then sighs. "Aren't you two getting tired of running from me?"

"We'll stop running if you'll stop chasing us," Chase offers.

"Then give me my suitcase back," he says.

"It's not yours," Ava says. "Madeline gave it to us after her uncle left it at her house."

"Finn had no right to take it from me!" Randall shouts.

Chase and Ava share a look. At least now they know Madeline's uncle's name.

Randall growls in frustration. As he does, the cube in Chase's pocket vibrates, almost like it's scared! Chase cannot let Randall take it.

"Time to go," he whispers to Ava. She gives a quick nod.

They turn and run toward the nearest moveable sidewalk.

"Hey!" Randall shouts, taking off after them.

It's easier for them to dart in between people and robots than it is for Randall since he's so big. Still, it takes another ten minutes of zigzagging through the streets before they're sure they've lost him.

"In here," Ava says, pulling Chase into a nearby store. They shut the door behind them and try to catch their breath.

A robot saleswoman rolls up to them. She is wearing a name tag that reads: Susie501. "Hello, Ava and Chase Teslar," she says. "Can I help you look your best today?"

"How do you know us?" Ava asks, moving closer to Chase. "We've never been in here before."

"Haha," Susie501 replies with a metallic-sounding laugh. "I have helped you two dress your best for *years* now. Follow me!"

Chase and Ava stare at each other. "Huh?"

# How Do I Look?

**chapter 5**

JUMP
SUITS
R US

SUSIE
501

***"I'm*** sorry, but you must be thinking of someone else," Chase says to Susie501. "We just got to town today." He can't believe he's talking to a robot!

Susie501 looks them up and down. "You do seem smaller now than at your last visit," she admits. "Do not worry, everything will still fit perfectly. What are you looking for today?"

Chase and Ava exchange looks. This is all *so* strange! But they can't stay in their pj's.

Ava finally says, "We need jumpsuits."

"Of course," Susie501 replies. "That's all we sell."

She rolls past them, and Chase and Ava get their first good look at the store. All the clothes are tiny, barely a foot in length!

"These jumpsuits would fit a doll," Ava whispers. "Are we in the wrong store?"

"I don't know," Chase whispers back. He glances at the other shoppers. They're all normal-sized humans, so that's a good sign.

The robot saleswoman plucks two tiny jumpsuits off a rack. "These would look lovely on you."

Susie501 ushers them to a full-length mirror.

A blue light inside the tall mirror scans them both up and down. An image appears of them wearing the jumpsuits!

Then something starts to happen to the clothes. The jumpsuits lengthen and expand!

Ava holds hers out in front of her. "It's the perfect size now!"

They duck into the dressing rooms and come out with big smiles. Their new outfits look *cool*!

Chase swings his arms. "So stretchy and comfortable! No wonder jumpsuits are popular in the future."

He sticks the cube and their pajamas into his bag and grabs their money. He holds it out to the saleswoman. "Will this be enough?"

Susie501 begins sputtering and sparking! Her head spins around! Smoke pours out. "Error," she squeaks. "Error."

Ava backs away. "Chase! I think you broke her!"

# Funny Money

## chapter 6

**A** crowd forms around Chase and Ava. "Where did you get paper money?" asks an older shopper in a loud voice. "I haven't seen that in *years*."

"I brought it from home," Chase answers honestly.

Other shoppers let out *oohs* and *ahhs*. Chase and Ava try to back away. The last thing they need when trying to hide from Randall is to attract more attention.

One woman says, "It's *greener* than I thought it would be."

A man says, "And *smaller*!"

"None of you have seen dollar bills before?" Ava asks.

They all shake their heads.

"Error . . . error," Susie501 squeaks again. Then she rolls off, bumping into walls.

"You better put that money away," a shopper in a pink-and-blue jumpsuit says. "You don't want people to think you stole it from the museum. They had a robbery recently." She narrows her eyes. "You didn't steal it, did you?"

Ava answers. "Of course we didn't."

Chase stashes the bills in his bag. "How do we pay without money?" he asks the woman.

"The usual way," she replies. "The robots scan your eyes to charge your bank account."

Ava and Chase exchange a worried look. They don't *have* an account.

Now that the money is out of sight, the crowd drifts away.

A different robot saleswoman rolls over to them. She holds sensors in front of their eyes. Their names instantly pop up in the air over her head!

They both reach out to touch the letters, but their hands go right through the image.

"Cooool," Ava says in a hushed whisper.

"Thank you for your purchase," the robot says, pushing them toward the door. "Come again." The door slams behind them.

"That was weird!" Chase says.

"Come on," Ava says. "Let's go shopping!"

Chase pulls her back. "There must have been a mistake back there. We can't just spend other people's money."

"But it's not *other people's*," Ava says. "Don't you get it? Susie501 said she knew us when we walked in. She must have scanned our eyes! And she said we looked smaller than usual. That means —"

Chase gasps as it hits him. "She really DID know us! Only she knows 'future us' . . . I'm over a hundred years old now!"

"So am I," Ava says. "Now let's go get a burger and fries, old man!" She points to a restaurant down the street. "I bet your favorite vanilla shake tastes even better in the future!"

"How can you think of food at a time like this?" Chase asks, though he does love a good vanilla shake.

But Ava is already halfway down the block. "Wait!" he calls after her. "What if 'future us' find out they got charged for clothes they didn't buy? They — I mean *we* — could show up any minute!"

She's too far away to hear him now. Chase quickly glances left and right to make sure Randall isn't lurking nearby. Then he hurries after her. But he can't stop thinking: Running into themselves would be SUPER WEIRD!

## chapter 7

# Fries with That?

COUNTER

RB

**"Welcome,** Chase Teslar," a robot host says as Chase enters the restaurant. "Please see the clerk at the counter. Your vanilla shake will be out shortly."

Chase stares at him. Can robots READ MINDS?

The counter clerk shouts out, "One order of 'the usual' for Ava Teslar."

Chase and Ava reach the counter just as a tray piled with a burger, fries, and a cup of milk swooshes out of a tunnel. It lands right in front of Ava! The clerk holds up a sensor in front of her eyes. Ava's name appears in the air.

"Awesome!" Ava says, popping a french fry into her mouth. "Chase, it's the coolest thing — they already knew what I wanted! I must eat here a lot in the future."

"That must be it," Chase says. He's glad to know that robots aren't really mind readers.

"Please take a seat," the counter clerk tells Chase. "Your order will be right out."

They find a booth in the back, so Randall won't spot them from the window.

A minute later, they hear, "One vanilla shake for Chase Teslar." A snakelike metal arm extends from the ceiling and places a tall, frosty drink on their table.

Chase takes a sip. *Delicious!*

"I could get used to this!" Ava says, leaning over to slurp her milk.

"The future is awesome," Chase agrees. "But we need to figure out what to do with this." He pulls the gold cube out of his bag and sets it on the table. "We don't even know what it is."

Then a squeaky voice says, "Yum! French fries! Can I have one?"

Ava pushes her fries toward Chase.

"I didn't say that," Chase says.

"Then who did?" Ava asks.

The same small voice says, "A vanilla shake! My favorite!"

"The cube is TALKING!" Ava exclaims.

Chase and Ava watch openmouthed as a little metal head pops out from the top of the cube. Bendy robot arms spring out from the sides!

The cube uses its hands to launch itself into the air as two legs pop out from the bottom. It lands on the table with a metallic creak.

"Ta-da!"

## chapter 8

# A New Friend?

*"**Hello.** My model number is A1205GBC4,"* the gold cube-turned-robot says as Chase and Ava continue to stare at it. "But my friends call me Jeeves. I am the very first prototype of the robots you see all around you."

"Our cube is . . . a robot named Jeeves?" Chase asks.

"What's a prototype?" Ava asks the little robot.

"I am the first of my kind. The result of decades of research," Jeeves explains. "I may not be as advanced as these other robots, but I'm the model for all who followed. I was getting awfully cramped folded up like that." Jeeves smiles, stretching. Then he pops a whole french fry in his mouth. "Yum!"

Ava shakes his tiny hand. "I'm Ava, and this is my brother, Chase."

"Lovely to meet you," Jeeves says. Then he tilts his head and squints up at them. "You both look familiar. Are you *sure* we haven't met before?"

"Positive," they answer together.

Jeeves squirts ketchup onto his elbows and knees. "I'm a bit rusty," he explains, stretching again. "Ah, much better."

"How did you wind up in our suitcase?" Ava asks.

"I am not certain," Jeeves says. "I was living in the Natural History Museum. I am part of a special exhibit called *The Dawn of the Robot Age*. Then four months ago a man with two different-colored eyes showed up."

Chase and Ava know exactly who that man is. "Randall!" they say at once.

Jeeves continues, "The man — Randall — must have deactivated me. The next thing I remember is that I started to power back up last night, in your suitcase. And now I'm here!"

Chase turns to Ava. "The cube powering back up must be what made everything in our house go crazy." To Jeeves, he explains, "Each object in the suitcase starts making noise when it's ready to go back to its own time. We don't know why. Or why in *your* case we fast-forwarded to the future."

"Wait, what?" Jeeves asks. "You're from the past?"

Before they can explain, a shadow falls over the table.

# A Common Enemy

## chapter 9

*"I'll* take that robot now," Randall says, reaching down.

"Escape! Escape!" Jeeves repeats as he scampers backward. Ketchup sprays out from his knee joints.

Chase quickly grabs Jeeves before he can get snatched up by Randall. He places him back in his bag. "Randall, why do you want to mess up history? And now the future?" he asks.

"You wouldn't understand," Randall says with a grunt. "Just give me the robot. Now! Then we can all go home."

"The robot has a name!" Ava adds, jumping up. Then she stomps on Randall's foot!

Randall howls and clutches his foot.

Chase and Ava don't wait around to see what happens next. They run past him and out the door.

"That'll slow him down," Jeeves says, poking his head and arms out of the top of the bag. "High five!"

Ava high-fives his tiny hand.

They don't stop running until they're out of sight of the restaurant.

"I wish we knew why Randall stole you in the first place," Chase says.

"All I know is that I need to get back to the museum," Jeeves says. "But I might get trampled if I try to go on my own."

"As Time Jumpers, our job is to return you to your rightful place in time," Chase explains. "We'll make sure you get to the museum safely."

"Can we use those flying roller skates?" Ava asks. "Or take a flying taxi?"

Jeeves shakes his head. "There's a faster way to get to the museum." He points to the metal rail high overhead that snakes across the city.

Chase feels dizzy just from looking up at it.

Jeeves rubs his tiny hands together with excitement. "We'll ride the Sky Train!"

# The Wrong Way

## chapter 10

**As** they near the station, Chase's stomach starts to hurt — and it's not from the vanilla shake. The train reminds him of a roller coaster he rode at the county fair last summer. He feels sick just thinking about it! The Sky Train doesn't have any drops or loop-de-loops, but it still goes superfast. He slows down until he's barely moving anymore.

"Why are you stopping?" Ava asks him.

"I, um, can't help looking at all the art," Chase says. The streets are lined with colorful murals, sculptures, and all types of 3D objects. He points at a large bookstore next to the train station. "And I'm happy to see there are still real books in the future."

"Oh yes," Jeeves says, his head still sticking out of the bag. "Ever since robots started doing the jobs humans would rather not, there's been an explosion of creativity — art, photography, writing, music."

"Our parents would love this," Ava says, peering at a moving sculpture. "What else have robots made possible?"

"Robots help people live longer," Jeeves says. "We keep people safe from accidents. We can tell when someone is sick before they start to feel bad and then heal them. We are also helping scientists search for life on other planets."

"Wow!" Chase says. "Have you found any yet?"

"We are very close," Jeeves says. "With people living longer, Earth will run out of oil and clean water one day. We hope to learn from other planets how they have survived. And I am very important to the space program! In order for scientists to reach these faraway planets, they will need *my* launch codes."

"What do you mean?" Ava asks.

"Scientists hid top secret launch codes in my programming because they knew no one would ever look in an old prototype like me," Jeeves explains.

Suddenly, a news alert appears in the air above Jeeves.

Robot prototype stolen months ago from museum is STILL missing! Space program will be shut down if it is not returned by
**NOON TODAY!**

Chase and Ava stare at him. "That must be why you were stolen from the museum!" Chase says. "Someone wants to stop the space program!"

"Come on," Ava says. She glances down at the cool watch built into her jumpsuit. 11:05. "We have less than an hour to put Jeeves back!" She dashes into the train station.

Chase follows her, forcing his fears of the fast train out of his head. If they don't hurry, Earth's entire future could be at risk!

A huge 3D map shows all the routes in and out of the city. But even Chase's skills with maps can't help him figure it out.

"I've got this," Jeeves says. He shouts out directions and they ride up in an elevator.

At last, Chase and Ava reach the right platform.

A train pulls up on each side. Passengers stream in and out of both trains.

"Which one do we want?" Chase shouts to Jeeves.

"We want —" Jeeves starts to say. But the doors to both trains are closing!

Chase and Ava grab hands and jump onto the closest train.

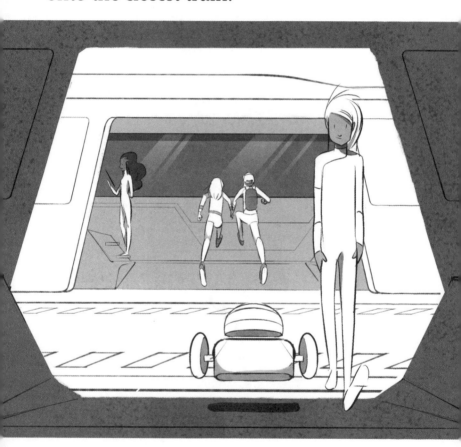

"— the other one," Jeeves finishes.

## chapter 11

# All Aboard

**"Oh** no!" Chase says, panicking. "We're on the wrong train! Now we'll never get Jeeves back in time!"

Jeeves pats Chase on the shoulder. "I was only joking. This is the right train."

Ava giggles at Chase. "You should have seen your face."

"Very funny," Chase says as the train glides along the track. Ava doesn't seem scared by their height or speed at all. She presses her face up against the window, so Chase does the same.

The view is amazing! There are only a few puffy clouds, so he can see all the shiny buildings and flying cars below them. It's too bad the train isn't going over their own neighborhood. It would be so awesome to look down on their house!

The other train passengers are talking about the same things people talk about in the past — school, work, sports. One little blond girl even reminds Chase of Ava when she was younger. She's fiddling with a small box around her neck while chatting with a robot friend.

The train finally pulls up to the last stop. Chase can see the Natural History Museum down the street. It looks exactly the same as back in their own time!

The doors open, and Chase starts to get out. Ava pulls him back.

"What?" he asks.

She points across the platform. Randall is here!

Chase's stomach drops. "If he reaches the museum before we do, he'll do everything he can to keep us from returning Jeeves."

"Don't worry," Jeeves says. "I know a shortcut."

# Back to the Museum

## chapter 12

DO NOT ENTER

***Jeeves*** points toward a tall door marked
DO NOT ENTER.

Chase opens the door and peeks inside.
"It looks dark. And dusty. And it says we
shouldn't —"

But Ava steps right through.

"Wait up," he says, scrambling after her.
The door leads into a snakelike tunnel. The
only light is coming from Chase's bag, but
he doesn't remember packing a flashlight.

Jeeves climbs onto Chase's shoulder. The light is coming from *him*. He's glowing! Chase remembers how bright the cube had gotten in the suitcase back home. That's a pretty handy trick!

"Here we are," Jeeves announces a few minutes later. An unmarked door in the tunnel leads right into the crowded lobby of the museum.

"Try to keep out of sight," Chase says to Jeeves. He doesn't want to have to explain to anyone why they have such an important stolen object with them. The robot slips back down in the bag so only his head sticks out.

Chase looks up at the dinosaur skeleton in the middle of the lobby. "Back in our time, this used to be a brontosaurus," Chase says. "When did this stegosaurus get here?"

"As far as I know, the museum has never owned a brontosaurus," Jeeves replies.

"That's weird," Chase says. "Our tour guide in the past said the brontosaurus was *such* an important find that it would be on display forever."

Just then, the little blond girl and her robot friend from the train run past them.

The girl goes up to an old man and gives him a big hug. Chase can't stop staring at them.

The man swings the little girl around. "Hello, Pippa!" he says. Then he glances over in Chase's direction and their eyes meet.

A shiver runs down Chase's entire body.

## chapter 13

# Me, Myself, and I

**Chase** grabs Ava's arm. "I . . . that's . . . he . . ." But all he can do is point at the old man, who has now turned back to the little girl.

Ava lays the back of her hand on Chase's forehead, like Mom does when they're sick. "You feel okay? You're not making sense."

"I feel fine," Chase insists. "Ava, that's ME! Me, in the future!"

Jeeves cranes his neck to get a look at the man. "That's Professor Teslar," Jeeves says. "He's in charge of my exhibit, *The Dawn of the Robot Age*. He tells a lot of corny jokes about history."

"Teslar's *our* last name," Ava says in a hushed voice. "And Chase knows tons of corny history jokes!"

"That's why I thought you both looked familiar!" says Jeeves, clasping his hands together. "I know your future selves!"

"I WORK AT THE MUSEUM?" Chase shouts joyfully. For a history lover like him, working in a place like this is his dream job! "I have to talk to him — I mean, to me."

Jeeves taps Chase on the shoulder. "You might not want to get too close to your future self," he warns. "If you bump into each other, it could be very bad."

"How bad could it be?" Chase asks. He really wants to go over there.

Jeeves shrugs. "Well, you'd most likely implode into a giant black hole, taking everything around you with it."

Chase stops short. "Okay, that sounds pretty bad," he admits.

Ava suddenly grabs Chase's arm. "Look at the little girl!"

"Pippa is your great-granddaughter," Jeeves tells Ava.

"Seriously?" Ava shrieks with joy. "And she's taking pictures with that tiny camera around her neck!"

"Just like her great-grandmother," Jeeves says. "Ava Teslar is — I mean, *you* are — a famous photographer now."

Ava's eyes fill with happy tears. Chase gives her a high five. Their future selves both have the perfect jobs! But right now they have to finish *this* job!

Chase and Ava keep an eye out for Randall as they run through the hallways. Most of the exhibits they pass are new, but at least the Egyptian wing hasn't changed.

They turn the corner, and voices call out from rows of robot-filled shelves. "Jeeves! Jeeves! You're back!"

Robots that look almost as small and old as Jeeves hop down. Jeeves climbs out of Chase's bag and jumps to the floor. His robot friends all start hugging him. Jeeves laughs.

Chase and Ava barely have time to catch their breath before Randall runs into the room! They dart in front of Jeeves and his robot friends in the hopes of hiding him.

But Jeeves marches right up to Randall. "You need to leave!"

"Oh, I'll leave all right, but not alone!" Randall grins and pulls out his remote.

"The remote won't send you home yet,"
Chase tells him. He glances over at a label
on one of the exhibit shelves: PROTOTYPE
A1205GBC4, ALSO KNOWN AS "JEEVES." "We haven't
finished our job."

But Randall continues to smile. He pushes
some buttons on the remote, and to Chase's
and Ava's surprise, the red button begins
flashing!

# Who to Trust?

## chapter 14

PROTOTYPE A1285GBC4
ALSO KNOWN AS
"JEEVES"

X-4547G    WW-23    @@-1-    /\X

**"Our** remote won't light up to send us home until *after* an object is back where it belongs," Ava says to Randall. "How did your remote do that?"

Randall waves his flashing remote in front of Chase and Ava. "I'll tell you if you tell me where the suitcase is!"

Chase crosses his arms and says, "The only person we'd ever give the suitcase to is its rightful owner — Madeline's uncle."

Randall sneers. "Haven't you wondered why Finn had a suitcase full of *stolen* items? Or why he was *fired* from his job at the museum?"

"He was fired?" Chase repeats. Madeline had told Chase and Ava that her uncle worked at the museum and that she doesn't know where he is now. She never said he'd been fired. Could this mean Chase and Ava have been keeping the suitcase from the wrong person? Chase has a sinking feeling in his stomach.

As though reading Chase's mind, Randall says, "Believe it or not, *I'm* the good guy. Not Finn."

"Could that be true?" Ava whispers to Chase, her eyes darting to Randall.

"Don't believe him!" a man's voice calls out. The robot crowd parts, and Professor Teslar and Pippa walk right up to them. "Randall is lying!" Professor Teslar yells. "*He's* the thief!"

Randall suddenly snatches Jeeves off the ground and lifts him high in the air. And he is still gripping his flashing remote!

Ava nudges Chase and points at Pippa's feet. Small wheels have popped out of the sides of Pippa's sneakers. Chase can hear a low whirring sound.

A second later, Pippa shoots up into the air! She's wearing flying roller skates! Before Randall can react, Pippa grabs Jeeves and zooms up to the ceiling!

Jeeves is safe! The other robots cheer.

Randall jumps up, trying to reach for Pippa. He doesn't even come close. As soon as his feet land, Ava acts fast. She darts forward and presses the flashing button on Randall's remote. She scrambles back and calls out, "Stand clear!" to a surprised Chase.

"Noooooooo!" Randall shouts. Then he vanishes into thin air.

# Two Peas in a Pod

## chapter 15

**Randall** is gone.

"Woo-hoo!" Ava and Chase cheer.

Pippa lands back on the floor, and Jeeves hops out of her arms.

"We make a great team," Ava tells Pippa as they beam at each other.

Pippa grabs Ava's hand. "Come see my favorite place in the museum to take pictures!" She and Ava head out of the room together.

Professor Teslar reaches out to pat Chase on the shoulder.

Chase shouts, "Wait! No! Don't come any closer!"

But it's too late. The professor gives him a gentle pat. Chase's eyes widen as he waits for the explosion.

But nothing happens.

Chase turns to Jeeves. "Giant black hole?"

Jeeves shrugs. "Hey, I'm just a prototype. I get a lot of things wrong. I'll leave you two to, um, get to know each other." He runs off to his old friends.

"So . . ." Professor Teslar says with a grin. "I got billed today for one jumpsuit and a vanilla shake. Would you happen to know anything about that?"

Chase's cheeks heat up. "I'll pay you — I mean *me* — back."

Professor Teslar laughs. "That won't be necessary." Then he says, "It was fun being part of the action back there. I've been helping the space program scientists look for Jeeves ever since he was stolen. When I saw you and Randall, memories of being a Time Jumper came flooding back to me."

Chase stares up at him. "How could you forget being a Time Jumper? I mean, I know you're really old, but still!"

Professor Teslar laughs again. "When you've lived as many adventures as I have, they all blend together after a while. But being a Time Jumper gave me some of my happiest memories. For a moment, it felt like I was right back in it again."

"So you must know why all the stolen items wound up in the suitcase?" Chase asks excitedly.

But Professor Teslar shakes his head. "At this point, I only know what *you* know."

At the same time, they both say, "Time travel is weird!" then crack up.

Ava and Pippa return. "Wait till you see the pictures I took!" Ava says as she snaps one of Chase and his future self. Probably best not to print that one out!

Chase looks at his watch. 11:57! He walks over to Jeeves. "Are you ready to go back into the exhibit?" Chase asks.

Jeeves nods.

Chase and Ava each take an arm and place him on the shelf where he belongs. They hold their breath, waiting for the familiar feeling of time stretching . . .

PROTOTYPE A1205GBC4,
ALSO KNOWN AS
"JEEVES"

## chapter 16

# Blast to the Past

**A** bright golden glow surrounds Jeeves. They did it! Jeeves is back in his rightful place in time.

"Ah, it feels good to be home," Jeeves says with a happy sigh. "Thank you both."

A new headline appears in the air:

The space
program is
SAVED!

PROTOTYPE A9999904,
ALSO KNOWN AS
"JEEVES"

Right on time, the remote in Chase's bag
begins to buzz. Chase and Ava take turns
hugging Jeeves as best they can.

Ava hugs Pippa, and Professor Teslar
pats Chase on the shoulder again. "Guess
it's time for you to go," the professor says.

Chase nods, his throat tightening up.

"I've got a riddle for you," Professor Teslar tells him as Ava pulls out the flashing remote. "If April showers bring May flowers, what do May flowers bring?"

Ava groans and presses the red button. The ground begins to spin.

Chase calls out, "Pilgrims!" He hears Professor Teslar and Pippa laugh as he and Ava swirl back in time.

*THUMP!* They land on his bedroom floor. The house is quiet. The suitcase is still under the bed from when they'd left earlier that same day.

Ava slides it out, and Chase puts the remote away. Then she shuts the suitcase again.

"I wish we knew where Madeline's uncle Finn disappeared to. It'd be great if he was around to explain things to us," Ava says.

Chase nods. "I know — that is, *if* he's a good guy."

They stare at the suitcase, wishing it could tell them its secrets. "Hey, look," Chase says, pointing at the stickers on the lid. "Maybe these are clues! We've time traveled to some of these places already."

"I wish we knew which place we'll time travel to next!" Ava replies excitedly.

And as though wishing made it happen, they hear, *thump thump bump bump.*

They look at each other and flip open the lid.

The uncooked potato is jumping out of its slot!

Chase grins and says, "I think we're about to find out!"

# WENDY MASS

has written several award-winning series for young readers including the **Willow Falls** series, *Twice Upon a Time, Space Taxi,* and *The Candymakers*. She recently learned that you can travel back in time every night just by looking up at the sky! The light from stars takes so long to reach us that any star you see is in the past. How cool is that? Wendy and her family live in a rural part of New Jersey. They have two cats and a dog, all of whom she calls her son's name by mistake.

# ORIOL VIDAL

is an illustrator and storyboard artist who lives in Barcelona, Spain, with his wife, daughter, and a cat named Lana. He always wanted to be a "painter" when he grew up. Finally, his hobby became his job! Time Jumpers is the first early chapter book series he has illustrated. When Oriol is not drawing, he likes to travel with his family all over the world. And in his dreams, he time travels to the past . . . just like the Time Jumpers!

# Time Jumpers

## Questions and Activities

### FAST-FORWARD TO THE FUTURE

**1** Chase and Ava's mom touches the flashing cube. What happens? Does she time travel? Why or why not?

**2** On page 40, Jeeves calls himself a **prototype**. Look up what this word means. Then explain to someone else what a prototype is.

**3** What will happen if Chase and Ava do not return Jeeves to the museum in time? Reread Chapter 10.

**4** Madeline's uncle Finn is the original owner of the suitcase. Turn back to page 76. What do Chase and Ava learn about Finn?

**5** Chase and Ava jump forward to the year 2121. They see robots and gliding cars in the future! What do you think the future will look like? Draw what you'll see there.